** DID I READ THIS ALREADY? **

Place your initials or unique symbol in a
square as a reminder to you that you have
read this title.

B.M			L	MW
				JW

THE BODEN BIRTHRIGHT

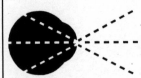

This Large Print Book carries the
Seal of Approval of N.A.V.H.

THE CIMARRON LEGACY

THE BODEN BIRTHRIGHT

NOVELLA

MARY CONNEALY

THORNDIKE PRESS
A part of Gale, Cengage Learning

GALE
CENGAGE Learning·

Farmington Hills, Mich • San Francisco • New York • Waterville, Maine
Meriden, Conn • Mason, Ohio • Chicago

GALE
CENGAGE Learning®

LIBRARY OF CONGRESS CATALOGING-IN-PUBLICATION DATA

Names: Connealy, Mary, author.
Title: The Boden birthright : novella / by Mary Connealy.
Description: Large print edition. | Waterville, Maine : Thorndike Press, 2016. | Series: The Cimarron legacy | Series: Thorndike Press large print Christian romance
Identifiers: LCCN 2016017907 | ISBN 9781410492050 (hardcover) | ISBN 1410492052 (hardcover)
Subjects: LCSH: Large type books. | GSAFD: Love stories. | Christian fiction.
Classification: LCC PS3603.O544 B63 2016 | DDC 813/.6—dc23
LC record available at https://lccn.loc.gov/2016017907

Published in 2016 by arrangement with Bethany House Publishers, an imprint of Baker Publishing Group

Printed in Mexico
1 2 3 4 5 6 7 20 19 18 17 16

THE BODEN BIRTHRIGHT

1

Boston, Massachusetts

August 1852

"Bad boy!" Grandmama Bradford slapped Cole's wrist. "You've sloshed tea on the lace of your shirt."

Tea on the lace of his shirt? What? Chance Boden felt like he'd taken the slap himself — with a ten-day-old, ice-cold mackerel.

When had his son started wearing lace?

He woke up at that instant to realize he'd been in a daze ever since Abby died. He'd loved her so much. Abby, precious Abby, dying in his arms. He never should have let her have another child.

The grief almost dragged him back under. The guilt. The emptiness. The pain.

The lace.

His eyes focused on his son. He had on pastel blue velvet short pants. His dark hair was in . . . in . . . God have mercy, it was in ringlets.

There were high heels on his shining black boots.

Cole, four, flinched at the slap and said in a cultured, quiet voice, "I am sorry for my carelessness, Grandmama."

What four-year-old talked like that?

When Chance was four, he'd lived in Indiana on the frontier. He'd spent his time trying to grab his pa's shotgun to shoot squirrels. Pa hadn't slapped him, either. He'd laughed and taught Chance how to fire the gun, then carefully hung it out of reach between lessons.

"I should hope so, young man. Your new shirt is ruined."

Chance opened his mouth to start yelling. To drag his son out of this room, and this house, and for heaven's sake out of that lacy shirt. He'd get the boy some proper trousers . . . and a haircut. The lace was bound for the fire.

Then he clamped his mouth shut,

stood, excused himself and left the room. He knew his mother-in-law, Priscilla, too well. Nope, if he started yelling he'd lose this fight the minute he started it. He had to do something radical and he thought of exactly what as he marched out of the mansion.

He'd always been a man who faced things head on. Being clear-eyed and fast-thinking had helped him get very rich in Boston.

Now he faced the fact that his in-laws would fight him for control of the boy who would be their only heir. And even considering that Chance was very well-off, his wealth wasn't a patch on Priscilla and Davidson Bradford. They had enough money and connections in

Boston to take his son from him.

So Chance didn't consider it an overreaction to decide to grab his boy and run. Take him somewhere the Bradfords couldn't influence lawmen and judges.

Indiana where Chance had grown up wasn't far enough.

He spent days making careful, quiet financial moves. He converted everything he had into gold. It was considerable because Abby was a wealthy woman in her own right, and Chance had done well working in business.

He found a wagon train leaving for the West. It was late in the year, so it was heading for St. Louis and staying to the south along the Santa Fe Trail.

Working through discreet agents, he bought three covered wagons, supplies to fill them all, mules to pull them, and tools to build a home when he decided where the trail would end. All under an assumed name.

Then he bought clothes for his son. Real clothes, not a stitch of lace or velvet anywhere. He packed the bulk of them, but kept one outfit along with a pair of scissors.

Chance hired good men to drive his wagons with his plans carefully explained. Chance didn't fool himself that Priscilla would make it easy. He knew her too well.

As he worked out the details, every evening Chance went home and ate supper like a good little boy, as obedient as Cole. When he made his move it had to be sudden, the break absolute. But the year was wearing down. By choice he stayed away when the wagon train headed out with his men and wagons.

Nearly two weeks went by before Chance's time came.

The wagon train was far down the trail. It could go about ten miles a day. He needed it to be a good distance from Boston before he joined it.

Priscilla and Davidson were leaving early in the morning for a weekend garden party with friends. There would be a buggy ride in the country to a big estate, and Cole wasn't invited.

Which was unusual.

Now that Chance's eyes were open, he realized Priscilla kept Cole at her side almost every minute.

The waiting had driven Chance half mad, and he'd avoided the house a good deal of the time to keep Priscilla from getting suspicious.

When Priscilla and Davidson left, Chance acted almost as soon as the dust settled behind them. He left a note saying he was taking Cole to the shore for two weeks.

Priscilla would assume he meant the Atlantic shore when in fact they'd be skirting Lake Erie.

No details beyond that. He sincerely hoped she didn't look for them until they'd caught up with the wagon train and were past St. Louis. Then if she hunted them, she'd be looking in the wrong place. With luck, by then he'd have well and truly lost himself on the Texas prairie. The woman had always been determined to control anyone who was within her reach, and her husband, Davidson Bradford, was worse.

They'd never had much luck controlling Chance. Abby had stood against them at Chance's side.

But they got Cole, because Chance was so buried in grief.

After the Bradfords left, Chance, not all that certain where his son's loyalties lay, said, "Cole, we're going for a ride in the park this morning."

The boy might tell the butler if Chance explained what was going on and then word could reach Priscilla within hours.

They rode out. Chance was careful to be on his own horses, not animals the Bradfords could accuse him of stealing.

Chance met a man in the park, who quickly traded horses with him, so that his own glossy, fine-boned thoroughbreds couldn't be described. Then Chance rented a room in a crowded boardinghouse. He only needed it to arrange a disguise. His and Cole's. He dressed them both in rugged wear fit for a long trip. Chance cut his son's hair and pulled a broad-brimmed western hat down low on his forehead.

"What do you think, son?" Chance held a very pretty brown curl up in front of Cole's eyes.

Those eyes gleamed in a way that gave Chance hope that his son wasn't hopelessly lost to the shallow ways of his grandparents.

"I like having short hair like you, Papa."

Chance hugged Cole close, and those small arms came around. Chance held him so tight he wondered if the boy would protest. But Cole nearly strangled him as he clung to his neck.

Finally, Chance pulled back, his throat feeling tight. "I love you, son. I have been bad to you."

"No, you haven't, Papa. You've just been sad."

"Call me Pa from now on, instead of Papa."

Cole tilted his head and a spark showed in his eyes. "Pa. All right."

Chance realized he hadn't seen such a lively expression since he'd begun planning their escape. It gave him hope that he could help Cole have a childhood again.

"I *have* been bad to you. I haven't spent time with you or talked to you like I should. It was sadness about your ma dying, but I have a fine son. I should have been spending time with you. You've needed me and I haven't been a good pa to you. That's going to change. You and I are going away where we can be a family again."

Cole blinked a few times, and Chance braced himself to be told by his son that the boy loved his grandparents more than he loved his pa. It was what Chance deserved.

"Can I stop wearing clothes that itch now, Pa?" The hope in the boy's eyes wrung a chuckle out of Chance.

"From now on you are going to wear clothes like these I just put on you. Clothes like the ones I've got on." They both wore brown trousers and a broadcloth shirt. They had boots — not high-heeled ones — and broad-brimmed brown leather hats. Chance had strapped on a gun belt. He was remembering who he was before he'd met and married Abby.

He was going so far west, God was going to have to come hunting him, let alone Priscilla Bradford. And Chance was going to go hunting God. He'd neglected God, as well as his son.

"We're going on a train ride, Cole."

Cole's dark-blue eyes were wide with excitement. Chance felt like he was seeing the real spirit of his son, the boy behind the careful manners.

"Let's go."

They left the boardinghouse and rode straight for the train station.

Chance had only a small satchel, for the bulk of what he owned was on that wagon train. The boy hadn't realized it, but the clothes and the horses and the haircut amounted to a disguise. Chance expected Pinkertons to get involved, and he'd done a fair amount to slip away. Probably they would be found eventually, but not for a while. Not until they were well outside of the range of Davidson Bradford's power.

The horses were going with them, so Chance and Cole oversaw them being loaded, then jumped on board. The train chugged out of the station within minutes of their arrival. A train to Lake Erie had just started running this year.

They'd take a riverboat to St. Louis and meet the wagon train there, or if, as Chance hoped, the wagons had reached St. Louis and gone on, he'd catch up to them riding horseback.

And then he'd raise his son right.

2

Chance had never seen anything so beautiful in his life. He knew without one speck of doubt that he was home.

White peaks in the distance. A vast pastureland dotted with a huge herd of cattle, ringed by rising hills covered in quaking aspen trees.

They'd been seeing the cattle and pastures for days. But today was the biggest herd of all, spread out miles in each direction with a perfectly built ranch house at the center of it all.

Mountains sloped up around the edges of the pasture. Aspen covered the nearly vertical slopes. Thousands of trees, each with yellow leaves sparkling and twisting like living sunshine.

He'd find the man who owned this house and ask where his borders lay and go just beyond. This was New Mexico, newly added to the United States and even more recently sliced off from Texas to form the New Mexico Territory.

It was a wild, beautiful land.

Looking at the expanse of rich grassland set against the grandeur of the mountains, Chance felt the stirring in his blood to give his son a birthright, to create his own dynasty, to be a conqueror.

The West was doing that to him. He'd noticed it as his hands blistered, then grew calluses. As he sat on the wagon seat in cold wind and burning sunlight. He loved rising to the challenges. The West was making him think bigger, dream of daring things. See what he could wrest out of the land with brute strength and the wits in his head.

But Chance fought the impulse.

He looked down at his son. Cole was his future. His goal in life was to be the best father he could be. No dynasty was going to tear his attention away from what was most important. His precious boy was staring wide-eyed at the mountains before them. Chance liked that the boy was paying attention to the mountains rather than the grand house. He liked that what shined in Cole's eyes matched what had to be shining in his own.

Chance planned to live in such a way that his son would grow up to be a strong, wise, honorable, faithful man. And the only way Chance knew to teach that was to be such a man himself.

This wagon train was going all the way to California, but as of this moment, Chance was at the end of the trail. The men driving his three wagons had already agreed to stop when Chance stopped. They all planned to work for him. In turn, Chance promised to help them put down stakes of their own. They were fine men, no doubt with ambitions of their own. If they didn't want to stay, Chance would wish them well and find a way to manage alone. His newly callused hand rested on Cole's head.

The boy tore his eyes off the view and smiled up at Chance. "It's mighty beautiful, Pa."

Chance talked to his men. If they wanted to go on, they needed to stay with the wagon train, which hadn't stopped. He'd give them one wagon and plenty of supplies plus their promised wages, and wave them on their way. But the men were as enthused as he was.

Chance and his men drove their wagons right into the ranch yard.

Chance wound his reins around the brake and hollered for his men to wait.

He took Cole along, and they walked up the five steps to the huge stone porch that wrapped all around the adobe-and-log house. Chance had seen plenty of humble homes as they drove along on the trail, but he hadn't even known you could build a two-story home out of the dried bricks.

As he realized how much he had to learn, he decided that starting a large ranch didn't have to be his first act. Maybe instead he could start small and learn the ways of New Mexico Territory. He wondered if this man might be interested in teaching him.

He knocked on the front door, and it swung open immediately. The residents of the house had seen him coming. And why not with three wagons and twelve big Missouri mules? He had a small herd of cattle, a crate with chickens and pigs — everything he could think of.

He forgot all about his wagons and cattle when the prettiest woman he'd ever seen stepped into the doorway, her eyes snapping blue, her yellow hair piled high on her head. She was tanned, which was considered unfashionable back east among the upper classes, but who could help but be tan in the relentless sun? She wore a fancy blue gown with lace at the sleeves and neck. It made him think of the velvet pants and lacy sleeves he'd taken from his son. He'd burned them, but they were just fine on her.

Despite the delicate feminine clothing, her expression was fearless and curious, and her eyes locked on his. He reacted so strongly he forgot what he'd come for. Only moments ago he'd thought the view of the mountains was unmatched for beauty. Now, with this woman, he had a new standard.

Then Cole tugged on his pant leg. She looked down and a smile bloomed on her face.

"Hello, young man. Who are you?" She spoke to Cole with a

musical voice.

Cole seemed to come alive under her attention. Chance knew what that felt like.

"I'm Cole Boden, and this is my pa, Chance Boden. We'd like to live here please."

Her smile faded as she looked up from Cole to Chance. "This land is ours."

Ours. So she must be . . . "Are you related to the owner?"

A huge bear of a man came up behind her, sounding like the most welcoming person in the world. "Ronnie, let 'em in."

The man had a full beard as bushy as fur, and his hair was overlong. He was pure muscle and stood about six feet tall, Chance's height, and wore brown broadcloth pants and shirt with red suspenders and heavily scuffed boots. No finery like his daughter.

Her eyes narrowed. "Look at them, Pa. They've brought supplies. I think this is another fool who wants to take our land."

The man's friendly manner shrank and hardened faster than adobe bricks in the noonday sun. "That right?" He looked past Chance to the wagons. "You think my land is free for the taking?"

Somehow Chance had gone from two welcoming smiles to being the enemy. "No, I do not."

Cole inched up against Chance's leg, and Chance rested his hand on his son's shoulder and spoke more calmly. "I'm Chance Boden. I'm looking to settle. My boy and I came west after my wife died, to start over."

Ronnie — which couldn't be this beautiful woman's name — looked down at Cole, and her expression softened.

"I saw this beautiful land, and when I got to your home, I told the wagon train to go on to California without me. What I'd like from you is to know the boundary of your property so I can settle nearby. I won't take property anyone else owns, but in this vast open country there must be a grassy valley some-where that's unclaimed. My men and I and my son would settle there."

The man studied him silently for a long stretch, taking Chance's measure. A man who trusted his instincts. Chance was sure that whatever he decided, his decision would be final.

The man finally nodded. His eyes didn't lose their watchfulness as he reached out a massive hand. "I am Francois Chastain. Call me Frank. We've had trouble a time or two, so I'm primed and ready for it. Come on in."

He shook Chastain's hand, which felt like cowhide. He nodded at the wagons. "Tell your men to unhitch. They can find food for the horses around back. I've got a bunkhouse full of cowhands who will help. There'll be food for your men there and a decent bed. You can all rest overnight, and I'll give you some directions."

"I don't want to put you to any trouble," Chance said.

"We'd welcome visitors, especially a young'un." Chastain turned kind eyes on Cole. "We don't see many children out here, do we, Ronnie?"

Ronnie gave her father an exasperated look. Her gaze swung to Chance. "My name is Veronica. No one calls me Ronnie except Pa. Come in. It's late in the day and we will have a meal in about an hour. There's plenty. You can wash up and talk ranching with Pa while I add two more plates to the table."

Veronica. A pretty name for a pretty woman.

"Much obliged, Frank, Miss Veronica," replied Chance. As he said her name out loud, he realized he hadn't really noticed a woman since Abby died. In fact, he hadn't noticed a woman since he'd met Abby six years back.

He was doing some powerful noticing right now.

"Let me talk to my men."

Veronica smiled at him. "I'll take Cole in and help him wash up."

"Thank you. I'll be right back."

His *noticing* felt like unfaithfulness. It was a pure shock to find a part of his heart he'd thought died with Abby was alive and kicking. To stop the reaction, he'd have wrapped Abby's memory around him and buried himself in guilt.

But he'd sworn to stop that. He needed to care for his son.

Since he couldn't let his thoughts sink into grief, he was left with not wanting to let Veronica out of his sight. She and Cole walked away. Chance turned to his wagons and went in the opposite direction of his son and that beautiful woman. It was one of the hardest things he'd ever done.

3

Veronica was so drawn to the little boy it surprised her. "Let me pour warm water for you while you wash."

Cole looked up at her and smiled. He was the most beautiful child she'd ever seen. His hands were grimy, as was his face. He had overlong hair, and she could see his clothes were coated in dust. She thought he looked underweight too, though how many little boys had she even seen?

Of course, they'd been on a wagon train. Certainly it was hard to keep clean, but everything in her wanted to help. She wanted to protect him and find him clean clothes and feed him.

She took up a cloth and washed days of trail dust off Cole's precious smiling face. She wanted to give him a bath, trim his hair.

"Cole, there is a cake in the kitchen, already sliced. Would you like me to get you a piece?"

Cole's eyes, a dark blue, widened with hunger. "Cake, miss? Oh yes, we didn't have many sweets on the wagon train."

Veronica set him up with cake and a glass of milk just as her pa came in, all washed up and rubbing his face with a towel. Veronica noticed for the first time the fine lines on her father's face. Lines that couldn't be put down to age. Pa was worried about something and had been for a long time. Yet he wouldn't discuss it with her.

Chance stepped into the kitchen. He dragged his hat from his head, his eyes going right for his son, which made Veronica's heart pang a little at his devotion. Most people who came here noticed the beauty of their home first. She never trusted folks who looked about them with awe and sometimes envy.

Then Chance's eyes came to her and, well, another pang. His son was the image of Chance, blue eyes and dark hair that had a bit of a curl. There was no denying they were both good-looking gentlemen. She looked away quickly, confused by her reaction. To fend off her unruly thoughts, she got very busy bringing Cole more milk and left Chance to Pa.

"Sit. I'll get you some coffee." Pa headed for the kitchen stove, a big cast-iron rectangle hauled here from St. Louis years ago, not long after Pa and his partner at the ranch, Don Bautista de Val, were given a half-million-acre land grant by the president of Mexico.

Then Mexico had sold this whole area to the United States in the Treaty of Guadalupe Hidalgo, and Don de Val was told that, to keep his share, he had to become an

American.

He was an arrogant man who took great pride in his pure Spanish blood and his close connections to the president of Mexico. Outraged, he went home to Mexico City. His half of the land grant was nullified, and Pa changed the name of his ranch to Cimarron after the river that ran though his spread. His cattle now had a bold twisted-together CR as a brand.

Frank had no qualms about changing his citizenship. Born in Canada, his mother had died when he was young and his father had moved to the American Rockies soon afterward. Frank had grown up there and stayed to trap. Because of the laws of residency, he was a full-fledged American simply by virtue of living in the country long enough.

He'd also done some wandering, and when he met Veronica's mother twenty-five years ago, he'd settled in this area while it was still Mexico.

He was temporarily riding with Don de Val when he managed to save the life of an important Mexican official. That earned him and the Don joint ownership in a Spanish land grant on the condition Frank became a naturalized Mexican citizen. Pa didn't give citizenship much thought, so he became Mexican and partnered up with the Don. After which the Don, a wealthy man in his own right, lived a life of wealth and ease on his half of the massive ranch, and Pa went to work and tore a fortune out of his half with the strength of his back and the sharp wits in his head. Then the land under them was made to be part of the treaty that changed it from Mexican land to American. The Don returned to Mexico City. And Pa, who'd changed countries so casually before, became American again.

At the time, it was a simple matter to be a citizen: just live in the country without committing a crime for a stretch of years and you were in. But despite the passage of more than enough years, the New Mexico territorial governor — or possibly men working in his name

— didn't care for the old land grants. They allowed Pa to be harried by settlers, who didn't recognize his ownership. The governor remained loyal to Pa because Pa was generous when the governor needed money. But Veronica suspected much was done in the governor's name that he knew nothing about.

And that could be the source of his worry.

Pa filled two cups with coffee, always kept warm on the back of the stove this time of year. "Ronnie, you want a cup?"

"Yes, thank you, Pa." Veronica enjoyed the cool weather of winter. It never got too fiercely cold, and it was a wonderful break from the brutal heat of summer. Besides, she wanted to sit and listen to the men talk. And she wanted to stay by Cole.

With the kind smile Pa used only with her, he poured a third cup. When he set it in front of her, the smile was kind, but there was something else in his eyes. His gaze shifted to Chance and back again, which reminded her that Pa had been known to do some matchmaking. She didn't take it seriously, however, not when they'd only met Chance a few minutes ago. Soon the four of them were sitting around the kitchen table.

"I haven't had much time to think, Chance, but it seems to me I can help you find a mighty nice stretch of land that might be just what you're looking for. There are native folks around, Pueblos mostly. They're peaceable folks for the most part. There are some Apache and Comanche, too. They can be cantankerous, but I treat 'em fair and get on with 'em well enough. I can help ease your way in dealing with them. We're a long way from anyone and we don't get much company. I like the notion of having a neighbor."

Chance smiled, and Veronica couldn't help but notice it was a fine smile. He was looking at Pa, but he glanced her way and she looked down quickly, embarrassed to get caught staring. What would he think of her?

"That is an offer I really appreci-ate, Frank. Is the land far from here?"

Pa leaned closer. He had a way about him when dealing with busi-ness. Veronica suspected Chance would be drawn in just as most men were.

"I own a quarter of a million acres."

"A quarter of a million acres!" Chance exclaimed. "I've never heard of a spread that big."

"Out here in the West there are plenty bigger than mine. One just to the north is four million. But I'm plenty satisfied with what I got."

"Satisfied?" Chance shook his head.

"My home is planted right in the

middle of my land, so the boundary lines are a ways off. And that's what I want to talk about."

Chance held his coffee cup with both hands, warming them on the tin, looking stunned at the talk of such huge tracts of land.

"What I'm wondering about is your boy."

Veronica narrowed her eyes at Pa. What was he up to?

A furrow appeared on Chance's forehead as his eyes flickered between Pa and Cole. "What about him?"

"Who's gonna watch after him while you're trying to tear a living out of this land? I'm established now, but I'll promise you it ain't easy — especially for a man alone and with a child to care for."

"The men who came in with me are going to stay, so it's not just the two of us. But even so, nope, not easy," Chance agreed. "I grew up on my pa's farm in Indiana. I tagged after him from a young age. Ma fed us, so I know she had a big part of caring for me, but I ran after Pa from morning to night. I expect Cole will do the same."

Chance looked at his son, who was listening to every word. He seemed like a mighty smart boy for one so young. "Won't you, Cole? We're going to count on each other."

Cole nodded. "We will, Pa."

There was a long silence, and again Veronica wondered what in the world Pa had on his mind.

"Here's my idea, Boden. I am always hiring cowpokes. But they're a rootless breed, always looking to the far horizon. In the winter it's not so much trouble to get by shorthanded, but I could surely use help."

Frowning as if confused, Chance said, "You want to hire me? I'm not looking for a job, Frank."

"Nope, you look like a man who is used to being his own boss and I respect that, but hear me out."

Chance nodded.

"A ranch in New Mexico Territory and a farm in Indiana aren't the same critter at all."

There was no reaction to that.

"My idea, especially because I

could use the help, is that you spend the winter here. Don't think of it as a job, though I'll be glad to pay you a decent salary." Suddenly Veronica was certain Pa was matchmaking, the old coot. "Learn about living in these parts. Get to know the land and how to handle longhorns."

"I've heard of longhorns, although I don't know much about them."

"Well, they're as hardy as scorpions and as mean as rattlesnakes."

"What's a scorpion?"

"A sort of huge bug that has a poisonous sting." Veronica was alarmed at the danger Cole would be in if Chance didn't have the sense to be wary of scorpions.

Chance's brows rose nearly to his hairline.

"If you'll spend at least a few months here, I'll teach you what you need to know about the good and bad in a rugged yet beautiful land. I'll help you scout out grazing and water holes that aren't claimed yet. I can teach you more about cactus, rattlesnakes, and which spider bites can kill you than you can believe. I'll show you where my boundary lines are and guide you to some prime grassland that's yours for the taking. You can find a place that suits you, with shelter from the worst of the summer heat. You can make a choice for yourself instead of letting me do the picking. I think you'll take to the land better if I ain't standin' by saying what you should choose."

Chance kept listening.

Veronica surely did like a man who wasn't bullheaded. Maybe Chance was such a man.

4

"I'm determined to be on my own, Frank." Chance tried to hide it, but inside, even though he'd considered that he could learn from Frank, every ounce of his stubbornness reared up at what felt like charity. Did Frank feel sorry for him? That didn't sit right.

Frank Chastain was a wealthy man, and something about the offer made Chance feel like a beggar.

And he wasn't sure how closely he wanted to associate with the

Chastains. This house was too much like his in-laws' place back in Boston. The lavish house was shocking in its finery, especially considering how far they were from civilization. All of it had been shipped out here, most likely at a staggering cost.

Making sudden decisions with confidence was one of Chance's best skills as a businessman and right now he made one. Though he wasn't looking for work, and intended to be his own boss soon, the only way he'd accept Frank's help was if he earned it.

"Instead of just letting me stay here and learn from you, I'll take a job. But I'll work hard for nothing beyond food and a place to sleep.

Learning will be payment enough."

Then Chance had a second thought. "I'm not sure Cole will do well in the bunkhouse. I don't know your men, so I apologize if I'm speaking unfairly, but sometimes the talk can get rough."

"I've thought on that, too."

Chance felt a flare of irritation. "You've done a lot of thinking for a man who's only known me for about half an hour."

Laughing, Frank said, "I've done more thinking than you can believe."

Now what in the world did Frank mean by that?

"But I'll put some of it aside for later. I've always had a housekeeper who lived here with us. The last one married my foreman, Sarge, a few months ago. I built them a house, so her rooms are empty. Consuelo still comes in every day, and her mostly grown daughter, Rosita, with her. But there are three rooms behind the kitchen that were hers. You and your boy can use them."

"I don't expect you to take me into your house." Chance felt his hackles go up again. "I'm a hired hand, and I'll live like one."

"I'm not doing it to treat you different from the other men," Frank said, waving off Chance's protests as if they were buzzing gnats. "I'm thinking of Cole, just as you are. I don't have a place fit for him in the bunkhouse. He can tag you all he wants, but if you ever have a chore that is dangerous to him, or when the weather turns bitter cold, which it does some days, you can leave him in here with my Ronnie."

Right when Chance had been ready to tell Frank to forget the whole thing, he mentioned Cole and danger and cold. He did need the help, but how much was too much? He'd left so much to his mother-in-law that he'd almost lost his son.

Chance reached over and covered Cole's hand. "I told you I'm not going to let anything keep me from being a good father to you, son. I left you to yourself after your mama died and I won't do that again. If I say yes to this, you'll live in a better place than if we build a rough cabin, but we'd work together."

As he said it, Chance realized just how young Cole was. A four-year-old couldn't do much.

"I can still spend time with you, even though we're living in here, can't I, Pa?"

That warmed Chance's heart. He was afraid the child's head might be turned by the fancy house.

"We surely will be together. I love you, Cole, and nothing is more important to me than showing you how much. Showing you every day."

"What do you say, Cole?" Veronica asked. She drew Chance's attention again, and he realized she was looking so sweetly at the two of them, almost like she had a mist of tears in her eyes. She was as pretty a little thing as he'd ever seen.

Giving himself a mental shake, he turned his attention back to his son. After so many months of neglect, Chance had too many fences to mend with his boy. He wasn't going to even think about a woman.

Cole shrugged and smiled. "We can stay, Pa. It's nice here."

Giving his permission, as if he understood how important his happiness was to Chance.

Looking between Veronica and Frank, Chance nodded. "I'm much obliged to you folks. Thank you, we will stay. And, Veronica, I would very much appreciate your help with Cole. He's a good boy."

Chance gave Veronica what he hoped was a look she'd understand was important. "Almost too good at times. He needs more time to be a boy. You won't fuss at him overly, I hope, nor keep him too quiet and still?"

Veronica looked down at Cole. "I'm not worried about a young boy being a bit unruly at times. And we'll find plenty of time to play."

"I'll have a meal on soon. Let me show you where you'll be staying. Then, Pa, do you want to show Chance around?" Veronica rose from the table and began picking up coffee cups.

Chance grabbed two cups and followed her to the porcelain sink.

Pa had poured the coffee. Chance was helping clear the table. She hoped Chance had a similar temperament to her father's.

She also hoped he'd let Cole stay inside with her all day every day.

5

Cole went outside with his father all day every day.

Veronica was impressed at the extent to which Chance kept Cole with him. But she was so charmed by the little boy, and he wasn't spending nearly enough time inside. Chance was out the door before Cole woke up, so she cared for him until Pa and Chance came in for breakfast. But then off he went with the men. After lunch, Cole usually slept for a time, and

Veronica got him for a bit after his nap. But then would come Chance to collect him again. Chance was showing great devotion to his son.

The big idiot.

She knew things were getting bad when she found herself hoping for bitter cold.

They'd been here the better part of a month now and Cole was as sweet to her as he could be. He was also rowdier than he'd been at first. She couldn't help but be glad of that. He'd been almost painfully polite at times.

They ate with the men while discussing land, cattle, riding, and roping. Cole talked too, and Chance was careful to listen to every word the youngster spoke.

Inwardly torn up with jealousy, she did her best to smile and listen to the day's goings-on, events she'd not been included in or invited to.

She realized she wasn't really listening when Pa said, speaking too loudly, "Ronnie, will that be all right?"

By his tone she knew he'd said her name more than once. "Will what be all right?"

Pa gave her an exasperated glare. "We're going to be out in rugged country tomorrow. Chance and I have decided it's too rough of a ride for Cole."

"Cole, will you stay with Miss Veronica?" Chance, consulting with his son. It was really sweet. It made her want to strangle Chance for giving the boy a choice.

Cole looked from Chance to her and back. "I'd be happy to stay inside if you need me to, Pa."

She was thrilled at the same time she wished Cole was spirited enough to throw a temper tantrum.

"Thank you, son. We'll be out for a long, hard day. Mr. Chastain is taking me to the high-up hills tomorrow. He says there are some mountain valleys that will make likely ranchland for us. We'll have to ride hard, though, because it's hours away."

Veronica's stomach sank as she thought of them living hours away. Why, she'd never see them again. Or if they did meet, she'd be nothing but a friendly neighbor.

Why was Pa finding land for the Bodens that was so far away?

Well, she'd have a stern talk with Pa soon enough, but for tomorrow, she got Cole all to herself. "What would you say to me baking a cake, Cole? We can have a special treat to celebrate your day here."

As if he didn't live right here. But still, she felt like celebrating.

"You know how much I love cake, Miss Veronica."

"Have you ever licked the spoon used to stir the cake batter?"

"No, back home I wasn't allowed in the kitchen."

That struck Veronica as strange. The kitchen was the heart of the family. "Well, you're allowed here in my kitchen. How can I watch you if you don't stay close?"

The boy's eyes shone like little bits of blue sky. "I'd even help if you wanted me to."

"I'd like that very much. Thank you."

She must have passed some test, because Chance started letting Cole stay in with her more and more. Or maybe the man didn't want his son to freeze to death.

It had turned cold. Regardless of the true reason, Veronica chose to believe the former.

Things were going well with Cole. Even Chance was acting friendly and grateful for her help.

The mystery was Pa. He had lost the matchmaking gleam in his eye, or maybe he'd learned to mask it. But those worry lines were still there, and she couldn't figure out how to erase them because he wouldn't talk.

And then Chance came in alone for the noon meal. Cole was in his room, fetching a clean shirt after he'd climbed on a chair and grabbed a gravy spoon. She was alone with Chance. Normally he and Pa came in together.

Chance looked around the kitchen. "Frank didn't get back?"

Veronica closed the space between her and Chance. His question startled her. "I didn't know he left. He's always with you."

"Not today. He rode out this morning."

"And he didn't say where?" Veronica had a bowl half-filled with mashed potatoes in her hands.

"Nope, he took off with barely a word right after breakfast. I asked if he needed help, but he said no and rode off to the south."

"Does he have part of the herd off that way?"

Chance shrugged, "He does, but he wouldn't check the herd alone."

"Pa's always preached to me that this is a rough country, full of dangers. Trouble can catch up to you in everything from a Comanche raiding party to a gopher hole that trips your horse. It's not safe for a man alone." Her worry grew as her voice rose. "He's the one who taught me that, and it's a rule

71

he enforces with the men and lives by himself."

Chance came closer, and their eyes met; she saw Chance's concern match her own.

"I shouldn't have come in with my worries."

"Please don't say that." Shaking her head, Veronica laid a hand on his arm. "I don't want to be sheltered against hard things. I've grown up riding herd more than most women, sticking to Pa like a burr, not as much as Cole sticks to you, but plenty. He's made me stay more to the house since I've grown up. He doesn't like the way the men pay attention to me, though they are always respectful. But I couldn't stand to stay in here if I thought the ranch work, the good and bad of it, was being kept from me."

Chance settled his hands on her upper arms. It was as if his strength were seeping into her, easing her fear. As the fear left, something else stirred deep inside her.

"I understand that. My wife and I never kept secrets from each other. Her mother was always trying to cause trouble between us, and Abby was too smart to give the old terror any room to cause a rift between them. Keeping secrets is one of the best ways to drive two people apart."

Perfect Abby.

Veronica hadn't heard much about her, but she'd seen the sadness in Chance's eyes. "I'm sorry you lost your wife. You must have loved her very much."

"I did indeed. I never thought another woman would . . ." Chance drew her closer.

She desperately wanted him to finish what he'd been about to say, since she was the only woman around.

Instead, he bent down and kissed her.

The shock of it and the sweetness were things she'd never prepared for. Never imagined.

"Pa, why are you so close to Miss Veronica?"

Shoving her away, Chance rubbed his mouth and turned quickly to his son. "Uh, I was just . . . uh, we were whispering. I needed to get close so she could hear."

"Whispering what, Pa?"

"That . . . that . . . I'm maybe going to have to miss the meal. Mr. Chastain needs me outside."

Veronica had her back to Cole, and a flash of irritation must have shown in her eyes because Chance, who'd been looking everywhere but at her, seemed to notice she was in the room and he glared. Or no, not glared. It was a different kind of strong emotion. One that warmed her and drew her.

"Your Pa has to ride out to find . . . I mean, to help my father." Veronica turned to face the little intruder. She loved this boy, but for just one second she rather missed the overly quiet child he used to be. And she wished he'd have just waited a few more minutes to come back.

"Your pa thought you'd be disappointed to have him miss sharing a meal. So we were whispering about what to tell you. But you're fine here with me, aren't you?"

Cole gave her a confused look, then his eyes slid to his father. "It looked more like you were kissing."

"Well, it was whispering, son. And now I've got to go help outside." Then, as if he'd gotten past that one foolish kiss, he said, "Sarge said your pa was real clear that we weren't to worry about him nor interfere with his business, and he'd be back by the noon meal.

Since we'd been working out back around the barns and corrals, I'd hoped he came in the front for some reason."

Now he looked torn between Pa's orders and all Pa had taught him. Chance seemed to be considering which set of orders from Pa to obey.

She actually caught herself wringing her hands, which was so unlike her it cleared her head. "Well, Pa's a knowing man. If he left on his own, he had his reasons."

"He, uh, he doesn't have a . . . a . . ." Chance's cheeks took on a reddish hue. He was blushing, and it was so fascinating, Veronica's attention was riveted.

So she didn't miss his meaning, he cleared his throat and asked sheepishly, "He doesn't have a . . . a lady friend, does he?"

Veronica inhaled so hard it was almost an inverted scream. "Pa? You think Pa snuck off to go courting?"

Chance held out both hands as if trying to halt her words. "I have no idea where he might be. But why does a man want to be alone? It occurred to me he might be meeting someone. And why would a meeting be a secret? I don't know your pa very well, but he seems like a man who says what he thinks right out loud. Not a lot of sneaking in him."

That was a fair description of Pa, for a fact. "So if he had a woman he was . . . well, visiting . . ." Veronica's mind was truly boggled. Pa had never shown a moment's interest in a woman since Ma had died.

Veronica felt like a child to have never thought of her father as a man who might want to marry again. Her own cheeks grew hot.

Chance shrugged, "I'm sure that's not it. We just need to be patient." He turned to look out the kitchen door and stood there with his back to the room for too long.

"No." His shoulders squared, and he whipped his head around, the blush gone, the awkwardness replaced by a take-charge man. "He should be here by now. I'm going hunting, taking the men with me. We aren't coming back without your pa."

Chance charged out the door and slammed it shut.

Veronica was glad Chance was going. Pa might be annoyed with a search party and people not trusting him to handle himself, but something was wrong about Pa going off like he'd done, and something was even more wrong that he wasn't back when he'd said.

She watched Chance stride away, with Sarge, John, and several other cowhands with him, thinking of how he'd touched her, remembering how he'd kissed her. There went a man she could trust. A sharp tug on her skirts drew her attention. She looked down at Cole.

His blue eyes were filled with confusion, also with affection. "So you were whispering with Pa and kissing at the same time? Why is that, Miss Veronica?"

And she felt her cheeks turning red again. "I need to check the pie I've got in the oven."

Cole's eyes gleamed with excitement.

"You go ahead and sit up to the table so we can eat." She was a very fortunate woman to have a child young enough to be distracted by pie.

6

"Over there! His horse!" John Hightree, one of the best cowhands on the Cimarron Ranch, a man Chance's age who'd become a good friend, spurred his mustang toward the gray stallion, standing with its head down. Unusual for Frank's spirited mount.

Chance was hard on John's heels, catching and passing him. Sarge only a pace behind.

The mustang started to lift its head, then lowered it again and shuffled oddly.

Slowing to keep from spooking the horse, Chance saw a rein tangled with the mustang's front leg. Had Frank dropped the reins and tripped the horse?

Chance got close enough to see beyond the horse. Frank's motionless body lay sprawled out on the ground.

Fighting back a shout of fear, Chance abandoned wondering about the gray stallion and went straight to Frank, swung down and knelt. The front of Frank's shirt was soaked with blood.

"Mateo, see to Frank's horse." Sarge's shout barely penetrated Chance's shock. "Monroe, you and Bud fashion a travois."

John skidded to his knees across from Chance just as he ripped Frank's shirt open.

They both looked at Frank's chest, then their eyes rose and locked.

Chance's voice was brutal, scraped raw. "He's been shot." Chance ripped his own shirt off, folded and pressed it against the ugly bullet wound high on Frank's chest.

John's worry switched hard and fast to rage. Chance saw him tamp it down and it helped Chance do the same.

Sarge crouched at Frank's head, took in the wound at a glance. The foreman pressed two fingers against his boss's neck. "His heart's beating. He's alive."

"He's lost a lot of blood." Chance was sickened by just how much.

Sarge's eyes snapped up. "Well, let's don't bury him quite yet."

Feeling the fury, Chance wanted to shout back. Slug someone. He and John looked at each other, then both turned to Sarge. They were all smart enough to know the enemy was long gone and there was no sense unleashing their anger on each other.

"I'll help get that travois lashed together." John leapt to his feet and was gone.

Chance didn't know much doctoring, but blood belonged inside a man, not out. He put his weight behind trying to keep what was left of Frank's blood where it belonged, holding Frank on this side of the Pearly Gates with his bare hands.

"Mateo, fetch a lariat off my saddle." Sarge barked at a steady young Mexican drover, a newcomer to the Cimarron. "We'll use it to keep pressure on the wound while we head for the ranch."

They had the rope in seconds, and Chance and Sarge used it to tie a bandage tight around Frank's chest, crisscrossing the rope over the wound. The only other way Chance could think to keep pressure on it was to walk alongside the travois all the way back to the ranch house. It was at least an hour ride and that was on a steadily moving horse. If a man had to walk, slowing the horse down, he feared Frank wouldn't live long enough to reach home.

John led a horse dragging a litter. "How's he doing?"

Chance said, "Someone needs to ride ahead to get Veronica. If she wants to see her pa again . . . she'd better come running. I know he's a strong man, but he looks bad."

Chance, Sarge, John, and Mateo, moving as smoothly as they could, got Frank onto the litter.

Once he was settled, Sarge said to Mateo, "Ride hard and don't go alone. Take Bud with you. Bring Miss Veronica here and have plenty of men ride as sentries. This might be a rustler Frank caught by surprise. But there's always those trying to take over Frank's range. If he dies, his daughter is in the way. Guard her as if she were your own sister."

"Sí. We *vamonos.*" Mateo jerked his chin, understanding bright in his black eyes of the danger to Veronica, of what it meant to bring her here, of what that boded for Frank. "We return *rapido* with Senorita Veronica."

Chance didn't even watch them go. He double-checked that Frank was solidly resting on the travois, and then he and John swung up on horseback, though everything in him wanted to run for the CR. Instead they walked at a fast pace, but anything quicker would be too rough a ride and most likely deadly for Frank.

Anyway, what more could be done at home? Chance didn't know the answer to that. And a rough ride might well shake Frank loose from the fragile hold he had on life.

7

"Senorita Veronica, come! You must hurry!" Mateo, one of Pa's cowhands, rushed into the kitchen right after Cole had fallen asleep. "Your padre is hurt. You must come."

Consuelo had just come in to help with the afternoon chores. Veronica looked at her. "I have Cole sleeping."

Consuelo said, "You go, *mia* Veronica. I will care for the *niño.*"

Veronica ran, terrified by the urgent way Mateo spoke and

moved. A horse was already saddled for her. She swung up and tore out of the yard after him. They rode south — the direction Chance said Pa went this morning. To the east of the CR was a tiny town called Skull Gulch, brand-new and barely existing. She knew there was no doctor there. None closer than Santa Fe, over one hundred miles away.

Sick at what Chance must have found, she bent low over her mount to get every ounce of speed. Then she focused her energy on praying. God had always been a steady presence in her life, and right now she needed Him desperately.

Hooves pounded behind her. She glanced back and saw five riders hot on their trail. Behind them a wagon was coming along as fast as it could, with armed riders on horseback as escorts.

What did they need so much help for? How bad was it? Questions jammed in her throat. She didn't ask them. She couldn't even consider slowing Mateo down.

It wasn't as long a ride as she feared. They saw three riders before a half hour had passed. Sarge, Chance, and John coming home. No sign of Pa. They wouldn't have left him unless he was dead. No, not even then.

Fighting back a scream, she dug her fingers deep into her horse's mane and bent so low over her saddle the pommel pressed on her chest. Her prayers went deeper and wider. She did her best to put her trust in the Lord. Whatever happened, she would let God guide her, even through the valley of the shadow of death.

And then she saw a travois behind John's horse. Pa, injured, but surely not dead. They draped dead men over a saddle.

She could breathe again.

Chance watched them approach until they nearly met, then pulled his horse to a halt and dismounted. Sarge and John leapt down, Veronica only a second behind them. John held all the horses, especially the one pulling the travois, so they wouldn't spook.

She rushed to Pa. When she

reached his side, she gasped at the blood. Horrified, she hunkered down by Pa and took his hand. Chance came to her side. They knelt there side by side, and it was a perfect time for prayer.

She'd said only a few words before Pa's hand tightened on hers. His eyes flickered open and went from her to Chance and back. Pa lifted his other hand, his whole arm and hand covered in dried blood. He reached for Chance.

When he had them both in his grasp, he said, "I'm dying, Ronnie. My precious girl . . ."

"No, Pa, don't say such a thing. We'll patch you up."

A sharp shake of his head was followed by a cough, and Veronica saw a tinge of blood on his lips. "Hush, girl, and listen."

Falling silent, Veronica prayed as Pa gathered his strength.

"I went to meet the territorial governor's man today. Fellow I've dealt with for a while. He's been riding all the way out from Santa Fe every few months, pressuring me to give over the rights to the Cimarron. He says I'm not enough of an American. I've been . . . been paying him. He has the governor's ear and will turn things against me if I don't —"

"Threats, extortion. If the governor knew . . ."

"Stop, Ronnie. Just let me get this out."

There was a long breath in and

out, so painful Veronica feared it might be his last.

"He claims it should go to American citizens. Chance, the only way to hold it, to keep it for Veronica, is if you marry her."

"What?" Chance wobbled, and for a moment Veronica wondered if he'd fall right over on his backside.

"Pa, you can't —"

"You'll do it right now, in front of me. With these men as witnesses. That is good enough for God, and good enough for New Mexico Territory. But I want more. You." He stabbed a finger at Mateo. "There's a circuit rider in Skull Gulch helping build an orphanage. I heard he's still in the area. Go for him and go fast."

Veronica saw something flicker across Mateo's face, anger at being ordered or maybe something else. For the first time she wondered if the young man had considered courting her himself. But no, surely not.

"Pa, we can't —"

"Tell him I want prayers," he continued, still cracking out orders to Mateo, "last rites, whatever it is parsons do at a time like this. We'll head on for the CR and meet you there."

Chance turned as Mateo mounted up. "Don't ride alone."

Ignoring the words, three men headed out with Mateo.

"Chance," Frank said, nearly crushing his hand, "please save the ranch for my daughter. I was hoping things would work out for you two anyway.

She was right — Pa had been matchmaking.

"I didn't want it to be like this, but —" An ugly cough shook his body and ended his begging.

And that's just what it was. Pa was the strongest man she'd ever known. To see him reduced to begging about rent Veronica's heart.

The coughing eased and Pa went on. "Now I want your oath, your solemn promise to a dying man." He looked from Chance to Veronica. "Ronnie, you love Cole. Chance is a fine man and strong enough to hold the land. Where will you go if you lose the ranch, Ronnie? You'll be forced to marry and it'll be sudden and possibly to someone who won't treat you right."

There was only silence.

The wait was too long for Frank. "Promise. Make your vows right here before God and these men."

There were still four riders who hadn't gone with Mateo. Sarge, John, and two others. At that moment the slower-moving wagon pulled up. The men reached for Pa to lift him.

"Stop. I won't be moved until I hear your vows, right now. If you lift me and I fight you, that'll finish me."

Chance stretched his free hand to Veronica. She took it and held on tight. The three of them formed a circle, with Frank holding both of them as they held each other.

"Will you marry me, Veronica? He's right that there is something between us. This is sudden, I know, but I will admit I've wondered if there could be a future for us. You are a fine, honorable, beautiful woman. It would be my great honor if you would agree to marry me."

Veronica only kept from shaking her head no by the increasing pressure on her hand by Pa. Finally, because what choice did she have, she spoke. "Yes, I'll marry you, Chance."

Without delay, Chance raised his voice. His words rang out strong and from the heart. "In front of

God and these witnesses I promise to be your husband, Veronica Chastain, until death do us part."

His words were solemn and carried the weight of a true vow to God.

She could do no less. "I swear this before God, my father, and all these men present that now and forever I will be your wife, Chance Boden. And I will honor you all of my life." She couldn't say love or obey. She just couldn't.

She knew on the frontier, when sometimes a parson didn't come around for years, many marriages started with such vows made before family. It wasn't unheard of for a parson to come by, marry a couple, and baptize a few of their children while he was at it.

Marrying Chance was an idea that appealed to her. And certainly after that kiss she'd hoped it appealed to him, too. But as he and Pa both said, not like this.

"Take me home." Pa cut into her thoughts. "I want to die in my own bed . . . after the wedding."

"But —"

"Veronica," Chance said, his voice achingly gentle, "let's get your pa home."

Chance's gaze met hers and she knew that whatever happened, their vows had been made and a promise would be kept. Whether Pa lived to see it or not, this day they would marry. They had in fact married already.

8

"What happened to Mr. Chastain?" Cole asked the question so grimly, Chance knew his son had come to care for the burly rancher. They'd done their best to staunch the blood and bandage him up, but Cole had to see how pale and wounded Frank was.

Frank had passed out on the painful trip home, and they tended his wounds as gently as they could, praying all the while. It had been more than an hour when his eyes fluttered open again. They'd been working over him on the dining room table.

He looked around. "Take me into the sitting room." Though Frank's voice was weak, his will remained strong.

Chance and John carried Frank to the room closest to the front door, a sitting room with fancy furniture. They settled him on a settee with deep-green tufted cloth covering it.

Veronica ran a hand over Cole's dark hair and drew him close to her side. Her affection touched Chance so deeply, he wanted to call it love.

He couldn't love her like he'd loved Abby. But her gentleness to Cole blended with the respect he had for her and he hoped someday it would grow into love.

"Where's that parson?" Frank said.

"Mateo's not back yet." Sarge took over the doctoring, untying the bandage, uncovering the wound.

With a frown, Sarge said, "Veronica, get your pa some water."

Veronica left to obey the order, as if desperate to help in some way. She took Cole along with her.

The moment she was gone, Sarge spoke quietly to Frank, "I can't cut the bullet out. It's too deep. My healing would kill you, Frank. If you want me to, I'll try, but —"

"We're old friends, Sarge. We both know what this wound means.

I won't have you cutting on me, making my last minutes on earth torture. Bandage it and get me in a clean shirt, then I want to see a wedding."

John rushed out for the shirt. Frank and Sarge spoke in low whispers as Sarge eased the bloody shirt off his friend's shoulders. Standing back because of the way the two spoke privately, Chance saw something barely peeking out of the front pocket of his boss's shirt.

When Sarge tossed the shirt aside, Chance caught it and checked. It was a good-sized slip of paper, smeared with fresh blood. There was also blood streaked inside the shirt pocket, which had a flap on the top and was snapped shut.

"Look at this." Chance's voice surprised him. He growled and sounded more animal than man. Sarge turned.

Chance extended the note to him.

"What's that?" Frank asked.

"This note was in your shirt pocket. Unless you put it there, whoever shot you left a message."

Frank's eyes narrowed. "It's not mine."

Sarge said something harsh that Chance couldn't understand.

Turning, Sarge handed the note to Frank.

Frank read aloud, " 'This is a warning. Clear out of this land you stole from Mexico.' "

Frank opened his mouth to say something just as Veronica returned. He thrust the note into Chance's hands. Sarge got back to work, getting a clean shirt on his old friend.

The men returned with the parson shortly after Frank was fully dressed and propped up in the corner of the sofa. "Someone said there's a doctor in Fort Union so I sent a rider."

To Chance it was the final death knell. The doctor wouldn't be here for hours and hours. Frank didn't have that long.

The parson, a thin, darkly tanned Mexican, rushed to Frank's side, knelt and began praying.

"I want your prayers, Parson, but first you need to hear some vows between my daughter and

Chance here."

The parson looked over his shoulder at Veronica and nodded with a worried smile.

Frank watched the wedding from a seat of honor, then welcomed Chance to the family by demanding he fetch a fountain pen and paper and listen as he dictated a new will, leaving his new son-in-law, an undeniable American citizen since birth, one of the old Spanish land grants that reigned over New Mexico Territory.

"But what about Veronica? She needs to be mentioned in the will, too."

"No!" Frank slashed a trembling hand. He looked at his daughter. "You understand why I'm doing this, don't you? I love you more than my own life. All I have is yours. But the law is hard on women, and you could lose this holding if it's in your name. Chance is your husband, and in the time I've spent with him I've taken his measure. There will be no mistreatment of you personally or of your land." Frank's voice faltered. "I leave you in good hands."

Pushing forward, Chance, with Veronica on one side and Cole on the other, dropped to his knees beside Frank to catch every word as he asked the question that had burned in him for hours now. "Did you see who shot you, Frank?"

"I won't speak of it. My daughter needs to be safe, and sending you on a dangerous manhunt won't accomplish that. Marrying Veronica to you will settle things."

"How will that settle things?" Then Chance shook his head. No time for anything but simple answers. "You left this morning to meet someone. Who?"

"Chance, protect yourself and my daughter and your son. I've endangered you, and I'm sorry. But I'm hoping this will thwart the scheme."

"What scheme, Frank? Tell me what you suspect."

"I won't. Talking won't save me and it'll put you in danger. I've protected Veronica with your marriage. Now give me a minute to say good-bye to my girl."

Veronica surged past Chance to clasp her father's hands. "Pa, don't talk that way. You've been hurt before. You just need time and good care and —"

"Let me have my say, Ronnie. Yes, with a miracle I might pull through, but I will spend the next few minutes making sure that if I don't make it, you'll hear of my love before I go. I am so proud of the woman you've become."

Chance eased back to give them privacy. They murmured to each other, and Veronica kissed him on the forehead, her tears baptizing him.

Frank then said, "Now let me pray with the parson, Ronnie."

Crying, she stood and backed

away until Chance held her, her back pressed to his front. She leaned so hard he was nearly holding her up.

The parson knelt again at Frank's side. Frank spoke first. "My faith is strong and my trust is in the Lord, so I have confidence where I will spend eternity. But I want to go on a prayer, with the Lord knowing I believe it is His will being done. I accept that it's my time."

Veronica was sobbing now. "No, Parson, pray for healing. Pray for a miracle."

The man glanced back at Veronica. "I'll do both, his wishes and yours. In the end it's the same — God's will be done."

His prayer was fervent and beautiful and soothing. The parson was still talking in quiet tones when God took Frank Chastain home.

9

It was early afternoon when Pa died, though Veronica felt as if she'd lived an eternity. The rest of that day was a blur of pain and loss and, for heaven's sake, marriage.

Veronica had cried until she was wrung out and numb. The sun set as her father was laid to rest, and now in the full dark she walked back from the family plot and noticed with some surprise that Chance had his arm around her waist. She was leaning nearly all her weight on him and wasn't sure she would have remained upright without his help. Cole was on her other side, holding her hand. He was so little, but he helped as best he could. Both of them maintained a solemn silence.

She barely knew them and now they were her only family. A new rush of tears flooded her eyes, when she thought she'd wept until she was a dry husk inside.

Pa rested under freshly turned soil beside her mother. His beloved Marie-Theresa. For all the elegance of her beautiful French name, Pa always called her Ma. Despite all his jumbled ancestry, Pa sounded like a western man from living in the wilds of the Rockies for a good part of his life.

And now it all belonged to her . . . and her new husband.

They were wealthy, she knew that, but it seemed like normal life to her. It had always been like this — the huge house, the lavish furnishings. Rich fabric in the chairs and drapes. Ornate carving on the curved staircases and woodwork. High ceilings and gilded mirrors. Beautiful artwork. Lushly thick carpets on the floors. Since Ma had died, Veronica and Consuelo had closed down sections of the house.

The ranch, the house, the wealth was all built by her father. A few miles away, on the half of the land grant Don de Val had owned, was another mansion that now sat empty. The proud Spanish Don's land had been split up between a few rough frontiersmen or reclaimed by the Pueblo and Apache peoples who'd roamed the land for centuries. No one knew what to do with a mansion.

Don Bautista was an arrogant old tyrant with a wandering eye, despite his equally regal wife. Pa had kept Veronica far away from him. It would be appropriate to write him of her father's death. One more thing she hadn't the strength for.

The weight of her long, sad day was pulling at her. As if she was to be pulled beneath the ground to stay with her parents. Mentally shaking the idea away, she found it creeping back in every few minutes.

Then she realized Cole was tugging on her hand.

Her thoughts were so dark, she welcomed the distraction. What if Chance and Cole weren't here? What if she had to face this alone? She held Cole's hand tight and cherished Chance's supporting arm around her waist.

"Miss Veronica?"

"You're to call her Ma from now on, Cole." Chance's instruction shocked her. She was a mother with a single spoken vow.

Cole smiled and said, "All right. Ma, do Pa and I sleep somewhere else tonight? Don't married folks pretty often share a bed?"

With a gasp, Veronica didn't respond. She hadn't allowed her thoughts to go anywhere near such a thought.

"They do, Cole." Chance answered for her. "But —"

"If you move into Miss . . . uh, I mean Ma's room to share her bed, where do I sleep? I don't like sleeping so far from you, Pa."

"Of course we'll . . ."

"Or are you going to come to Pa's bed?" Cole cut him off.

"Now's not the time —"

"Pa will want you close at hand, right, Pa? That's how a pa and ma sleep. So you can move into the rooms we're in. We'd have a good chance of finding you that way. The house is bigger than Grandmama's, and I got lost in there all the time."

"Cole!" Chance's voice was

enough to silence the boy. "We are going to give Ma a little time to rest. This has been a sad day for her. She doesn't need a single new thing to worry about. So tonight she will sleep in her room and we will sleep in ours, and we will talk about such things as moving when Ma is rested."

Cole looked so subdued that Veronica was tempted to tell Chance to leave the little boy alone. Even though Veronica desperately wanted him to be quiet and she was grateful for Chance stopping the inquisition.

And then she thought of her room, right next to Pa's, so far from Chance and Cole. Hesitantly she asked, "Would it be all right if

I slept in your rooms tonight? I don't want to be alone —"

Her voice broke and her knees sagged, until Chance swept her into his arms. "We'll do whatever you want, Ronnie."

Hearing her father's name for her brought the tears again. "Th-thank you."

She knew she was thanking him for carrying her, agreeing with her, and calling her Ronnie.

Chance strode toward the house, Cole at his side. He leaned close and his lips touched her temple as he whispered, "I will take care of you. You're safe. You're not alone."

Somehow it seemed as if those were his true wedding vows.

■ ■ ■ ■

Chance carried her straight to his room. He didn't even want to see the rest of the house. Every inch of it was a painful memory for Veronica. She shook with tears, silent and huddled against him. He'd been attracted to her spirit and fire from the moment she'd opened the door to him.

Knowing how strong she was made her grief all the worse.

He carried her into the larger of the two bedrooms and laid her on his bed.

"Don't leave me alone." She gripped his arm so hard he felt her nails claw his wrist through his shirt.

He had no intention of staying. She wasn't ready to share a bed with him. It would be an intrusion at a time like this. But neither could he rip her hand free and leave her crying in the dark.

Cole came to his side, his worry for his new ma stark in his blue eyes. Chance gave his son a long hug and said quietly, "Can you get into your nightclothes, Cole, and slip into your bed?" Chance had a flicker of amusement as he remembered his son's questions about Ma and Pa and beds. "I need to stay with your ma for a while. I'll be in to say good-night as soon as I can."

With heavy-lidded eyes, Cole yawned, nodded and left. It was hours after his bedtime, so the boy would be asleep in moments. He wouldn't notice if Chance was slow in tucking him in.

He had a moment alone with his wife. At last. And she needed him. With one arm still in her grip, he pulled her close, hoping his touch would give her comfort.

"I will stay as long as you want, Ronnie. I won't leave you alone."

She wrapped her arms tight around his neck, and he either had to fight her or move closer. Unsure if it was wise, he kicked his boots off and slid into the bed beside her.

"Just for a while, Chance, please. I need someone to hang on to."

It was too perfect to deny. He hadn't been near a woman in nearly two years, not since months before

Abby had died. She'd been bed-ridden during most of her pregnancy.

The feeling of such a lovely woman clinging to him was pure temptation. But not all temptation led to sin, not when he was forced by her terrible grief to hold her. Not when he was possibly falling in love with a woman he'd had no intention of marrying, at least not quite so soon.

He shifted his weight until her head rested on his chest. Her grip was so tight, there could be no thought of his getting away.

And truth be told, he had no interest in getting away anyhow.

He hadn't turned on any lights. His hands had been too full as he'd carried her in. Cole was almost certainly fast asleep and would call out if he needed anything.

And holding Ronnie was pure bliss.

It was beyond his ability to resist one gentle good-night kiss. She jumped just a bit as if he'd startled her, but she didn't pull away. Instead, one of those arms around his neck tightened while the other slid forward until she rested a hand on his cheek. She offered the next kiss freely.

The brief kiss they'd shared in the kitchen, perfect except that Cole had cut it short, was alive between them.

After far too long he ended the kiss with great reluctance. Her warrior's grip lessened as she shifted to lay her head on his shoulder. Her breathing slowed and settled.

He let her warmth lull him to sleep.

10

Veronica woke up and didn't know where she was. Then the cutest little guy she'd ever seen leaned over and stared at her, so close their noses almost touched.

"Good morning, Ma." Cole smiled as if those words were the finest ever spoken.

Her heart wrenched as she remembered yesterday's sadness. And then she realized Cole was hers forever now.

I lost my father. I gained a son. And

oh, my dear heaven, I've gained a husband! A husband who kissed me until I forgot my own name. Which — she had to think a minute — *is Boden. Veronica Boden.*

Drawing in a steadying breath, determined to go forward somehow and fight the tears always near to hand, and figure out how to be a good wife and mother, she reached for Cole's little-boy shoulders. She inched him back just far enough so she could sit up, swing her legs around, and stand.

"Wait in the hall while I get ready for the day, please."

He scowled. "I want to stay with you, Ma."

She was glad to see that tiny flash of childishness. He was turning more and more into a normal little boy, or at least what her notion was of how a boy should be. She had no experience.

She looked down at herself and realized she was already fully dressed, right down to her boots. A wrinkled mess, but perfectly modest.

Smiling down at him, she realized this sweet boy was her life now. He gave her purpose. He gave her something to do every day, which she hoped kept her from sinking into grief.

He and his pa were her family. Which reminded her of just how eagerly she'd responded when Chance kissed her. In fact . . . she glanced at the bed and saw two indentations, one on each pillow. Chance had slept here. She'd kissed him and clung to him, so glad for something to drive away her sadness. And then he'd held her close, and it was such wonderful comfort that she'd curled up in his arms.

Yes, she'd not only gained a son but also a husband, and so far that wasn't such a bad thing. Shocking, but not bad. Of course, it'd only been one day.

"Is your pa around?"

Cole grinned and gave a quick up-and-down shrug. "I don't know. I woke up and came to see if you were awake. He isn't here."

He'd made very certain she was awake, the little imp.

"Can you give me just a few moments to change, Cole? I'll be right out."

"All right, but hurry, Ma. I'm hungry." He dashed out of her room, slamming the door behind him.

Veronica's smile held as she made short work of washing up, smoothing her hair, and choosing a clean dress. She hurried from her room and found him two feet from her door, wriggling impatiently and grinning.

She offered him her hand, and he took it without a moment's pause. "Let's go. We'll get breakfast on and hope your pa comes in to eat. Judging by how high the sun is, he may have given up on me and gotten on with his day."

■ ■ ■ ■

"Chance, Sarge has something to say," John said, approaching Chance in the barn, who was forking hay to the milk cows. John jerked his head at the ranch foreman.

Sarge was a solid man who'd earned the respect of every cowhand on the ranch. He was an old trapping buddy of Frank's and he'd come out of the mountains to see his old friend and then stayed. Sarge had seen a lot, and Chance took what he said seriously.

"Let's step away." Sarge rested a hand on Chance's shoulder. "John, I want you to hear this, too."

The men were doing morning

chores. The Cimarron had pigs and chickens, sheep that kept them in wool, tame cows for milk. All in addition to the wilder cattle that earned the money and supplied plenty of beef. The animals Chance had brought west with him had all gone into their pens with the others. Even his men had joined with Frank's men and made friends and seemed to be part of the group.

Chance remembered that urge he'd felt to build a dynasty, to leave a legacy for Cole. Now he had this huge ranch dropped onto his shoulders. His few cows and chickens were nothing compared to all he'd just inherited. He was glad to protect Ronnie's land for her, but he still hadn't seen what he could do himself.

He wasn't experienced enough to run such a big ranch, and depending on Sarge and the other hired hands was proof of that. He was determined to learn all he could as fast as he could.

In the barn, there were men working all around. To not speak in their hearing meant Sarge didn't know who he could trust and that twisted Chance's gut.

"I rode with the cavalry for years; that's where my name came from. I did some Indian-fighting and saw a lot of the West before hardly a white man was out here."

Chance just listened. Not time yet to ask questions.

Sarge's eyes suddenly flared with

rage. "I've seen my share of gun-shot wounds and I worked with a crew of men who investigated such things. The bullet that hit Frank told me a story. You are assuming he was shot from cover and fell from his horse, but that's not the way it happened."

"The slug didn't pass through," Chance said. "Any close-up shot would have had an exit wound."

Sarge scowled impatiently. Chance wished he'd kept his mouth shut.

"There are guns small enough they don't use much powder, don't have much speed nor power behind the bullet. But up close they're deadly enough. Those guns are easy to hide in a coat pocket or up a sleeve. So a trusting man, even a knowing one like Frank, might not go for his gun before it was too late."

"So whoever shot him might have gotten close?"

"Not *might* have. He *did.*" Sarge looked around to make sure they were alone. "Someone was standing facing Frank, close enough to be talking to him. He pulled a gun and fired. The way the blood flowed — not only that but the way Frank talked at the end — he knew the one who shot him."

Chance had that same impression. "Why wouldn't he tell us?"

"He wanted to keep his daughter alive. He was busy doing that, getting a marriage arranged. And he did say something to you, didn't he?"

"I asked him who did it. He wouldn't tell me. He said it might put me in danger. His only thoughts were for Veronica and her safety."

Sarge said, "I asked him, too. He said to leave it be. All he wanted was to protect Miss Veronica . . . pardon, I mean Mrs. Boden."

"Why wouldn't he want his killer brought to justice?" Chance rubbed the back of his neck and shuddered in the blustery cold wind. "Why not protect Veronica that way?"

"Frank was dying," John said, "and I don't trust all the words of a man in such terrible pain. And he was so worried about his child.

139

Regardless, I want whoever shot Frank to hang. And I don't intend to let things stay as they are."

Sarge looked from John to Chance. "I agree."

Nodding, Chance said, "We're going hunting, men. Sarge, you're as good a tracker as there is. Let's ride out together and see if we can follow some tracks."

"I'll do it, and John can come along, but not you."

That surprised Chance, the way the old-timer gave him a direct order. But Chance didn't argue with him. Sarge was foreman, so he ordered men all the time. He was too savvy, too trail-hardened to ignore. He'd earned a little obedience, even if he was the boss.

Sarge continued, "You stay close to the house. Call it being newly married. Call it mourning, whatever you like. To my way of thinking, if someone shot Frank, and if the motive was to gain possession of the Cimarron Ranch, then you might be next. And I don't have time to watch over you today."

That tricked a smile out of Chance. It really was true that he probably needed watching. He was a newcomer out here, and for all that Frank had taught him, he was still the least knowledgeable cowboy on the place.

He wasn't completely useless, yet the men couldn't know that he was a better than decent shot, thanks to his childhood, a skill honed by hours at a shooting range back in Boston. He'd missed his country life more than even he had realized, and shooting had kept him in touch with the survival skills he'd had as a youngster in Indiana.

That same reason had sent him to a boxing club at least once a week where he sparred with some fine boxers and held his own.

Roping a calf was beyond him, though, and they hadn't branded cattle back east on his farm, but he understood livestock enough and could handle all the critters on this ranch. The business world he'd moved in had been cutthroat, yet he'd learned how to play a hard game without selling his soul. And his toughness combined with honesty had taken him far in Boston.

It had also taught him how to organize men. He knew how to lead. And he knew how to admit it if he couldn't handle something. All those were skills he intended to use to win the respect of every hand on the ranch. But by western standards, he was still a little soft.

And soft didn't survive long on the American frontier.

"All right," said Chance. "I'll stay with the family, at least for today. But I'm not hiding, Sarge. You can mention to the men that I've got heirs back east, powerful family members who'll own this land if I die. And who'll avenge my death."

He thought of the Bradfords and doubted they'd care one whit if he died. But Cole . . . yes, if something happened to their only grandchild, they'd bring every ounce of their power west to avenge him. And if Cole was alive, they'd move heaven and earth to find him and take him under their wing.

And by law, as Cole's closest relatives, the Bradfords would inherit. A modest holding wouldn't interest them much, but a quarter of a million acres and a vast herd of cattle? They knew money and they'd be greedy enough to want it all. So there was no way someone could gain this land by murder. Frank really had protected his daughter.

A spark of respect flared in Sarge's eyes and he nodded. "Git on back to the house and your new bride. We'll talk more after John and I have spent time at the place where Frank was shot."

11

Veronica got a fire roaring in the cast-iron stove, put coffee on to boil, and started heating up two skillets. Next she saw to a beef roast for dinner and set bread to rising. Meanwhile, Cole asked her questions constantly. He dragged a chair across the floor and climbed up on it and nearly leaned against the hot stove. Veronica found herself scrambling to keep Cole alive.

With dinner well under way, she turned her attention to breakfast.

She noticed the half loaf of bread she had was now gone. She was glad Chance hadn't gone out on an empty stomach.

She made short work of getting biscuits in the oven, then sliced side pork and dropped it into a hot skillet with a sharp sizzle and a cloud of steam. While the pork fried she broke eggs into a bowl and whipped them with a fork. When the pork was near to done and the biscuits just turning light brown, she dropped eggs into the second skillet. The eggs hissed and popped as she turned them and cooked them through.

As the kitchen filled with the smell of fried food and the roast began to give off a savory aroma, she began scooping up breakfast. She set a platter of biscuits beside another of pork and eggs, then poured milk into Cole's tin cup. She set a glittering bowl of red jelly on the table along with a ball of butter.

She'd made a mountain of food, thinking wistfully that Chance might come in. Most likely it would go to waste, for it had become too late for a working man's breakfast.

As she chastised herself for sleeping so late and missing her husband on the first day of her married life, the back door swung open. Thinking Consuelo had come, she looked up.

It was Chance.

His breath flowed out and formed

a small white cloud around his head in the cold air. He seemed to be preoccupied because he never looked at Veronica or Cole while he hung up his broad-brimmed hat and the heavy buckskin coat Pa had helped him make — right down to shooting the buck and tanning its hide.

He turned to the table, and his eyes locked on her and he froze. She had a strong suspicion he was just now remembering that he'd gotten married.

Chance had been so deep in his thoughts of all it meant to be married to Veronica that he hadn't noticed his honest-to-goodness, avowed-before-God wife.

All he'd had on his mind was how to keep her safe . . . to such an extent he hadn't been looking where he was going.

A good way to get shot. Considering what had happened yesterday, and the things Sarge had said, that was all too real a possibility.

All of this boiled inside him when he stepped into the house and saw his wife sitting at the table, caring for his son.

She smiled and leapt to her feet. "You're in time to eat. I thought I was too late to serve you breakfast, but here you are." She hustled toward him and slipped past to swing the door shut. He'd left it gaped open while he thought a few shockingly married thoughts.

This beautiful woman, tending his child and making him a meal, stirred his heart and burrowed through a wall of pain left from Abby's death.

"It smells wonderful, Ronnie. I found some bread this morning but didn't want to make any noise. You and Cole got a late start on sleep."

They stood, too close, watching each other, Chance remembering their kiss and . . . well, he could see it in her eyes that she remembered as well.

With a sassy toss of her head, she said, "Come on in and eat, husband. I even started coffee and it should be done and ready for you by now."

"Sarge ordered me to spend the

day with my new wife." He took her arm as if he were walking her down an aisle — there'd been no such thing at their wedding — escorting her to the table to sit straight across from Cole. "And let me bring you the coffee. You've done so much already."

"Hi, Pa. We hoped you'd come in to eat."

The kitchen was warm and smelled wonderful. Chance had been out working since dawn, and only now did he realize how hungry he was.

It was a homey room and not overly large. It didn't fit with the vast elegance of the rest of the mansion, and in the time Chance had been here he'd noticed the

Chastains spent most of their time in this room. Frank had an office, and they had bedrooms of course, but the kitchen was the heart of the home.

The table sat against the wall on one side. Frank and Veronica always sat on the two ends facing each other, Chance sitting on the long side to Frank's left, with Cole between him and Veronica. Now Frank's chair was empty. Chance averted his eyes from the chair, because it hurt to think that boisterous, hardworking man was gone.

Chance poured two cups of coffee from the heavy tin pot and then set it back on the stove with the scrape of metal on metal.

Inhaling the hot, rich scent of the

coffee, Chance served Veronica first then settled into his usual chair. Veronica passed the platters of food.

When their plates were full, Veronica said, "So Sarge sent you in, did he?"

Smiling, determined not to speak of Frank or yesterday's sorrow, Chance stabbed his fork into the mountain of fluffy scrambled eggs. "He didn't seem to think he'd have a bit of trouble managing without me. And he said a newly married man ought to spend a day with his wife."

"And with his son too, Pa?" Cole asked.

"With his son for sure." Chance mussed Cole's hair, and his boy, who'd given up most of the fussy ways his grandmama had taught him, scowled comically and smoothed his hair back into place. The boy did love to be neat. And maybe that wasn't his grandmother's doing, but rather just natural to the child.

"What shall we do today, Ronnie?" Chance found he liked having a special name for his wife. "Should we move to different rooms? Although I didn't mind last night's . . . arrangements." He resisted the urge to say *sleeping* arrangements, yet he was sorely tempted.

She looked down at her hands in her lap and spoke just above a whisper. "I didn't mind them either."

"Then let's stay in my rooms for the time being. It's simple and I think we should keep everything simple for a time."

"So I was right about a ma and pa sleeping together, wasn't I?" Cole piped up.

Chance was tempted to gag the little chatterbox.

"You were most certainly right, Cole." Ronnie looked up, and her cheeks were blushed a beautiful shade of pink.

"I remember you and my first ma always slept together. I crawled in bed with you one time and you were so close together it was like one of you was on top of the other. One time —"

"Cole!" Lowering his voice from a shout, Chance added, "Please, let's just finish breakfast."

Chance remembered the time and was shocked to realize Cole remembered it. There was a very good chance that their second child had been conceived that night. Cole would have been little more than two at the time. It certainly wasn't something he wanted to talk about in front of his new wife . . . or his son for that matter.

Ronnie had gone from pink to red-cheeked in the blink of an eye. These two were going to give him all he could handle for the rest of his life.

He planned to enjoy every single minute of it.

12

The morning was half gone by the time she'd cleaned up after break-fast, but they'd gotten a late start. Chance helped in the kitchen, and she found his closeness so distract-ing, she barely caught herself when she put the milk in the cupboard. When she quickly retrieved it and put it in the icebox, she found the saltcellar in there beside the flour.

She glanced at her husband, and he was grinning at her. She felt another foolish blush. He'd been

watching her all morning and working alongside her, though he was
no hand in the kitchen. Cole kept
up his talking and that somehow
added to the intimacy, made them
a true family.

Consuelo came in with her mostly
grown daughter, Rosita. She was a
good friend to Veronica. Rosita
hugged her, and Consuelo con-
gratulated them on their marriage
and asked Cole if he'd like to help
her bake cookies. The three of them
set to work.

Veronica wasn't quite sure how it
happened, but she soon found herself shooed out of the kitchen and
alone with Chance. Of course not
for the first time since their marriage, as they'd had last night after

all, but this was different. Exhaustion wasn't pulling at her now.

"Let me show you the house and decide which rooms will be yours."

"Wait, Ronnie." Chance reached out and took her hand.

She turned to face him.

"I want you to know that . . . well, last night I didn't intend to share your bed. But I think it was right that we were together. But holding each other is a long way from being . . . being . . ." He swallowed hard. "Well, it's a long way from being together as man and wife. I'll give you all the time you need. But I don't want my own room. I would like to sleep by your side. It's one of the great comforts of marriage to have someone with you so you don't have to face the night alone."

Since Veronica wanted him close with all her heart, it was simple to agree. "I do want to share a bedroom. But I'd like to know you better too, Chance. I've watched you work alongside Pa. I know you're a hardworking man, and I've only seen honesty and decency from you. Still, I'd like to know what brought you here. We see folks go by on wagon trains all the time, and they're always hard-pressed folks. Scrawny horses, few supplies, and no money to buy more. You have three loaded wagons. Hired men. Cattle and healthy mules. You're a prosperous man. And that's not the kind who strike out into the Wild West."

Chance was so quiet that Veronica wondered if she'd done wrong to ask. Surely now he'd speak of his wife and how he loved her and drive home to Veronica that she should never expect to replace the love of his life.

"I headed west because I needed to get my son away from that life before it ruined him."

"What life?"

Tugging at her hand, Chance said, "Come on upstairs. We'll decide what rooms to take, and I'll tell you about the woman who wanted my son to drink tea and wear lace."

Gasping, Veronica came along eagerly and listened. His story included his grief, but it also included him choosing to face forward, to put his mourning behind him, to make his son the center of his life. How he'd sold his company, laid down a false trail, and slipped away in secret.

"Didn't you once say you grew up on a farm in Indiana?"

"I did." More and more, Chance was taking on the speech of the West. Veronica had seen it before. Men out here could come from all over, not just in America but from all over the world. Her own father was born in Quebec, Canada. Don de Val was a Mexican citizen, but had spent many of his growing-up years in Spain. Though the Don was a bad example, because he'd always spoken Spanish and clung rigidly to his arrogant upper-class accent.

The West drew men who had the courage to face risks. Some who didn't feel fully alive unless they were pushing themselves to the limit of their strength and skill.

These men picked up the accent and slang of the West quickly, and only in the background could someone hear where they'd sprung from.

At times, Veronica could hear the East in Chance's voice, but after long days on the wagon train, he'd already shed much of that cultured sound. It was easy for a woman who loved the frontier to imagine a man wanting to come here. But how had he gotten to Boston to begin with?

So she asked him.

Smiling, Chance replied, "When I was growing up in Indiana, that was the far frontier."

"It's nearly on the Atlantic Ocean, for heaven's sake." They walked hand in hand up the stairs.

"It seems so from here, but there are mountains between the ocean and Indiana. Dense woods with rugged trails passing through it. It was a wild land. I grew up running in the hills, hunting and fishing, learning to track, learning the ways of wild creatures. I loved that part of our lives, but I had an older sister who married young and Pa took her husband into our farm. We needed to find more land to make a living for me. I could have done that, settled nearby, but I was restless. I wanted more. For some reason 'more' to me back then meant the city."

Veronica listened intently as she led the way to the rooms she thought were the right ones for them.

"Ma had family in Boston, a brother with some cousins a bit younger than me. I moved out there where Uncle Paul worked at a bank. He got me a job there and I really took to it. Somehow the numbers suited me. I could hunt for them like I'd hunted wild game, learn all their tricks, track down things that didn't add up."

"I'm a decent hand with hunting

and tracking myself, Chance." She smiled at him, and he returned a grin that said he knew and he respected her skill. It was the finest feeling in the world, after all the men who'd come calling, thinking she was a pampered princess in a castle. "Go on with your story."

Chance looked like he'd rather pay attention to her. "I found a knack for making sound investments. I built that into a business and made a name for myself that led me into some high social circles. That's where I met Abby. Abigail Bradford, from one of the snootiest families you've ever seen. They had roots that went back to the *Mayflower* and they never stopped boasting about it. But Abby was down-to-earth, the kind of sensible woman who'd have probably survived on the *Mayflower.*" Chance smiled affectionately, and Veronica tried not to let that pinch.

They were nearing Ma's long-abandoned room, and Veronica decided they'd talk about practical things like moving furniture and such, rather than about his dearly departed wife.

Chance stopped her from entering the room. He slid his arms around her waist and pulled her close. "I find myself in possession of another fine woman. No man has any right to be so blessed in his life. I consider myself a very lucky man to be married to you."

He bent his head slowly, giving

her all the time she wanted to ob-
ject.

She did no such thing.

13

The afternoon was fading away. Chance looked out the window of the room Ronnie said she wanted for them, with a smaller room right next door for Cole.

November was waning, the grass had faded to brown, and the yellow leaves were gone from the aspens. Days were short now, with the sun low in the sky behind a flat-topped butte that stood like a reigning king looking down on them all. Skull Mesa, they called it. It was nearly of mythical status because it had never been climbed, and Frank had told some funny stories about how, fresh from the rugged Rockies, he was sure he could climb anything. Even so, he became frustrated over and over as he tried to get himself to the summit of Skull Mesa. Then his old trapping buddy Sarge had come and they'd begun the whole futile effort again. The hired hands had tried. Many others had taken up the challenge too, going back as many years as folks could remember. All had failed.

Chance treasured the day with his brand-spankin'-new wife. He felt like God had given him this day to restore his soul and to form a solid bond with her.

Consuelo and Rosita had taken charge of Cole most of the day, and Chance had let Ronnie order him around, moving furniture and setting up rooms for the three of them.

They had deliberately avoided any talk of Frank or the shooting, time enough tomorrow for the trouble that loomed over them. Trouble so big it made Skull Mesa look like a gopher mound.

He thought the day was going to end as pleasantly as it had begun, until Sarge hollered up the stairs, "Chance, Miz Veronica, get down here."

Veronica smiled as she smoothed the bed they'd made up for Cole. "You're his boss, aren't you?"

Shaking his head, Chance said,

"I'm taking orders just like the lowest cowhand. Let's go."

They walked down the broad staircase to find Sarge pacing in the hallway below. Any humor faded as Chance realized Sarge was here to report his day of tracking. He regretted that this had to intrude on such a fine day.

They followed him into Frank's office. There was a settee and several overstuffed chairs. Chance wasn't about to go and sit at Frank's massive oak desk.

"What did you find, Sarge?" Chance pulled Veronica with him to the settee where they sat close beside each other.

"It ain't good." He sat down in a chair straight across from them, then surged to his feet and began pacing again. "I don't have proof of it yet, but I've got enough pieces I have to suspect it."

"Just tell us what you think," Veronica said.

"The tracks were pretty stirred up by the time we built that travois and all our horses milled around where Frank fell. But we found a single set of tracks riding out of the aspens to meet Frank. The man he met must have been someone he knew because they both dismounted and stood jawing for a while. We found one of those Mexican cigars tossed into the dirt, as if they'd stood there long enough for a smoke."

"Did you recognize the boot

prints or the hoofprints?" Veronica asked.

Chance knew a skilled tracker could identify a man from his tracks, a horse as well. But it wasn't that easy. Most men wore boots. Most horses were of a similar size and weight and were shod.

"I don't have to recognize them, Miz Veronica."

Chance's stomach twisted at Sarge's tone. The man was about to say something he didn't want to say, and Chance was sorely afraid that neither he nor Veronica wanted to hear it.

"Ramone's gone missing."

"What?" Veronica sat up straight at the mention of one of their best cowhands.

Chance leapt to his feet. "You suspect Ramone of shooting Frank? But he was here at the ranch yesterday morning." More thoughtfully, he added, "But not when we searched for Frank."

"Once we found he was missing, I started asking questions. You know how many cowhands are drifters?"

That much was true. They rode from ranch to ranch, worked a while, through roundup or through the winter, then wandered on.

"I just assumed Ramone was, too. But a few of the hands said he grew up around these parts. They said it was never spoken of, but a few of them knew Ramone's ma was a woman who —" Sarge cleared his throat — "who spent time with Don Bautista de Val."

"Spent time?" Veronica's brow furrowed as she stood and went to Chance's side.

Chance rubbed a hand on his chest. "Are you saying . . . ?"

"I'm saying Ramone is the Don's son. Born to a woman other than his wife. Ramone's ma was a kept woman all his life. The Don gave them a decent home with enough money to live well. He visited Ramone's mother right up until he went back to Mexico. Since he left he's had nothing to do with them, and the money stopped. Ramone came to the ranch hunting work, and" — Sarge glanced awkwardly at Ronnie — "some of the men knew because he'd spoken of it. He had plans to marry you, Miz Veronica."

With a gasp, Veronica touched her fingers to her throat.

Chance added what was most likely also part of the plan, an ugly part. "And by doing so, get the Cimarron. He no doubt thought this should have been his family's legacy. He gets by marriage what he was denied through the circumstances of his birth."

Veronica asked, "Did Pa know about Ramone? That he was related to the Don?"

Sarge rubbed his hand over a chin stubbled with a week's worth of beard, considering. "If he did, I never heard of it, and your pa talked most things over with me. But what I'm wondering is if Ramone faced him with it yesterday."

"If Ramone asked to talk with him, Pa wouldn't have thought twice about getting down off his horse."

"What's more, Ramone is a fiery one. He has a temper, and I've seen it explode a few times. But mostly he's a top hand and a hard worker. If the men are right that he had plans that included you, Miz Veronica, well, there was no way to miss that your pa was taken with Chance here. Ramone might've thought he needed to speak up, ask for your hand, or at least your pa's permission to court you before Chance was taken any more under

Frank's wing."

"You think Ramone suggested he be allowed to see me and then shot Pa when he refused?"

"This is all just talk." Chance slid one arm around Veronica's waist, wishing he'd heard Sarge's story outside. "Ramone might just as well have confronted your pa about being Don de Val's son. He might have asked your pa to hand over half the remaining ranch out of some twisted notion of fairness."

Sarge's scowl twisted into fury. "I plan on hunting Ramone down, and when I find him I'll ask him just what he said before he shot Frank."

Ronnie reached out and rested her hand on Sarge's broad shoulder. "No, don't do that. Don't go hunting him. We need you. Consuelo and Rosita need you."

"I know your pa, Miz Veronica. He wanted to protect you. If your pa had lived, he'd have fought this. But knowing he was dying, he only thought of the danger his death would leave you in. And the danger to Chance if he'd go to hunting a killer. By marrying you to Chance, he protected you should Ramone try to further his plans after Frank's death. But that was a decision made by a dying man. I'm alive and I'm not going to let some kid shoot down my friend in cold blood and ride away free. I'm going after him."

"Sarge," Chance interrupted, "I

don't think he had any plans to kill Frank yesterday. He was angry and his temper exploded. I suspect he's run far and fast. If he's made it to the Mexican border, you've lost all legal power to bring him to justice and you will put yourself in terrible danger. That's what Frank was worried about when he said telling us the name would put us all in danger. No lawman or posse has any rights once they cross the border. In fact, I'd imagine Ramone ran to his father in Mexico City. You'll never catch up to him before he's among folks that speak his language and may be inclined to protect him."

"And if in a fit of anger Ramone shot a good man like Frank," Sarge added, "then he's as dangerous as a rattlesnake, because he's one ugly temper away from killing again. We need to lock him up and hang him before he kills another innocent man —" Sarge paused, gave Veronica a grim look — "or woman."

Silence hung over them. Sarge was right, but Chance was right as well. Sarge was risking his neck with very little likelihood he'd catch the youngster, certainly not before he reached the border. Because if Ramone had ridden hard and fast, he was in Mexico already.

"I reckon you can go after him if you've a mind to, Sarge. You're your own man. But I wish you wouldn't. We need you here. You know with Frank gone, that is

God's honest truth."

With a glint in his eye, Sarge said, "Let me scout around. If I find out Ramone made it to the border, we let him go."

Chance fought down the urge to go along. "I'm worried about running this place without you."

"I'll send out a group of my best trackers," Sarge said, "and I'll ride along. I found his trail headed south. We'll see if he's quit the country or is just hiding out for a while."

Breathing out a sigh of relief, Chance nodded. "Be careful. And remember your home is here and we'll be waiting for you. Don't stay on the trail too long."

Sarge gave one hard downward

jerk of his chin. "I'll have a word with Consuelo and Rosita, then be going." He raised his dark eyes and looked at Veronica. "You know I've watched you grow up with as much pride as if you were my own child."

"I know." Veronica came forward and curled her delicate fingers around Sarge's scarred thick-fingered hands. "Please don't be gone too long. I need you here on the Cimarron and I *want* you here, because I think of you as family."

A light blush pinked up Sarge's heavily lined face, and he managed a wry smile. "I'll be back, Miz Veronica."

"You've never called me Miz before in that buzzy way. It was always Miss Veronica, even though I'd told you many times that wasn't necessary. Why are you saying it different?"

Sarge managed a much fuller smile on that question. "It's just a quick way of saying missus. I reckon it should be Missus Boden, but it's hard to change from saying Veronica."

Veronica leaned forward and kissed one of Sarge's reddened cheeks. "Be careful and hurry home."

Sarge spun away, charging toward the kitchen as if the gruff old cowpoke was afraid he might show a soft side of himself.

14

Chance looked at Veronica and thought of how bravely she'd taken such devastating news. "I am sorely tempted to ride with him."

"But you're not going to?" She sounded hopeful.

"Nope. I'm staying at your side." He walked right up and caught her face between his palms, caressing her temple and brow with his thumbs. "I am the luckiest man alive to be married to you, Ronnie. I intend to spend my life making sure you never have cause to regret being my wife."

He leaned in and kissed her as gently as a breeze. He wanted only tenderness between them. The time for passion would come later, though Chance now knew it wouldn't be long in coming. When he ended the kiss, he rested his forehead against hers and closed his eyes.

"I have spent my time here on this ranch very much aware of how beautiful you are. I've always known you were brave and strong and suited to this land in every way. But only today did I see you're as sturdy as . . . as Skull Mesa."

"You just called me a massive butte."

Chance kissed her just to make her stop talking. And probably best for him to stop, too.

When he needed to breathe again, he spoke just the barest inch from her lips. "I said all that so you'd understand why I love you, Ronnie."

A soft gasp slipped from her swollen lips. "You love me?"

He smiled and snuck in another kiss. "How could I not? When I've been blessed with such a woman as my wife, every moment spent not realizing I love you is wasted."

Her hand slowly crept up his chest, then her second followed more quickly. "I love you, too. And for me there are no reasons, though you're a fine man. For me, there is only the way my heart beats faster when you enter a room. And the simple fact that no man has ever made me so aware that I am a woman."

With a nearly silent groan, Chance said, "You are that."

When their next kiss ended, Ronnie asked, "How long would you say we have until Cole wakes up?"

The question seemed out of place, but Chance said, "After his short night's sleep last night, I reckon he'll be out for a while yet."

Something blazed in Ronnie's eyes. "You told me I could have all the time I wanted before I share myself with you as a woman does with her husband."

"You can," he said solemnly.

"I believe I've waited long enough."

He smiled, then laughed out loud as he swept her into his arms and carried her up the stairs.

EPILOGUE

"Justin is punching Cole again." Chance sounded weary at the howl of outrage coming from the other room.

All of Cole's overly proper behavior was gone now. He still had a liking to be neat and had taken to books at a young age. He was five years older than his little brother, Justin. So Cole had no trouble outrunning him.

"I'll go break them up," Chance said. "You stay there and rest."

Ronnie rocked in her chair and smiled. It usually started out as horseplay. Then someone, usually Justin, got too rough and it stopped being fun between them.

She looked down and adjusted the blanket so that her precious newborn daughter, Sadie, didn't get a chill. It was January in New Mexico Territory and the days were cold, especially for a three-day-old baby.

A girl. She grinned wider, thrilled to add a daughter to her precious family.

Cole howled louder.

Precious but noisy. She asked, "Does Justin ever actually land a punch?"

"If he has, Cole's not afraid to

holler."

"Nope, no sign of that. Besides, if he really got hurt, I'm not sure Cole wouldn't punch back." Chance left the room and was back in a minute with three-year-old Justin in his arms.

Cole followed, looking smug. He knew that, being eight years old, he could never really fight a little brother half his size. Instead he ducked and dodged. He had doors with knobs out of Justin's reach. Cole could open, get through, wait and taunt Justin, then slam the door in his face. And when Cole got tired of it, he just fell over on top of his little brother to pin him down until he surrendered.

And for the perfect amount of

fun, Cole was quick to make a racket that brought Ma and Pa to help out.

Ronnie was a lot slower to come to the little imp's rescue since Sadie's birth. In truth she loved seeing Cole's behavior. He'd given up all his proper Boston manners and become a boy again.

Chance did his best to take the boys along all the time. Justin could already ride a horse, though usually Chance carried his son in front of him when they rode. Cole was a fine rider and could even saddle his gentle mare with just a bit of assistance.

"You don't think Sadie will grow up punching the boys, do you?" Ronnie asked.

Shaking his head, Chance looked down at the tiny scrap in Ronnie's arms. "I'm sure she'll be just as genteel and ladylike as you were when you were little."

Ronnie groaned. "I was a terror."

Chance laughed out loud as he sat in a rocking chair beside Ronnie. They enjoyed the fire and the temporary peace. Which came mainly from having Justin distracted.

Cole came up and stared at the baby. "She's so little, Ma. Was I ever that small?"

Ronnie exchanged a worried glance with Chance. Cole didn't seem to remember anything of his life before New Mexico. They never spoke of Boston or his overbearing grandparents or the fact that he had a mother besides the one he knew.

"You were the size of any new-born baby, Cole. Just like Sadie. And she'll grow just as you and Justin have."

They could have lived their whole lives with Cole not knowing his past, except they'd gotten another letter from Boston just this week. One of many. The Bradfords had spent years tracking Chance down, and they'd finally found the Cimarron Ranch and written with their intentions of sending the law to retrieve Cole.

It was a nuisance, but she didn't see how they could succeed. Ronnie's family was good friends with the governor and they had consulted with judges; they had the law on their side. Which set Ronnie to worrying about illegal methods.

She knew Chance kept a close watch on Cole when they were outside and was mindful of any new cowpokes that hired on. He'd told her he didn't put it past the Bradfords to send a Pinkerton agent in disguise to spirit their grandchild away.

They also had Sarge and John on alert. It was a well-run ranch, and the Bradfords would find they'd kicked over a hornet's nest if they tried to take Cole.

As they shared this peaceful moment, Ronnie thought back to the way they'd married, to the death of her father, to the ranch her husband found thrust into his hands. She knew he'd wished to build something of his own. She couldn't help but smile as she looked at Cole and Justin and Sadie. This was their finest accomplishment. These three children would be their legacy.

Thinking of Pa made her ask, "Did Sarge ever hear back from the Mexican government about Ramone?"

"Nope, and I reckon he never will. After all the times he's traveled down there, we have to accept that Ramone has gone into hiding, probably protected by his father. It doesn't suit me to give up, but as long as he stays in his country, we can't get justice for your pa. I'm sorry, Ronnie."

"I've never wanted to arrest him at the risk of more lives, Chance. You know that. I'd worry if I thought he was still around, a threat to us. But I won't push for bringing him in if it endangers you or Sarge or any of the men who'd ride with you."

Nodding, Chance said, "It's between Ramone and God now. He'll answer for what he's done at the Pearly Gates."

"In the meantime we'll have a good life." Their chairs were side by side. They creaked gently as they rocked. Cole clambered onto Chance's lap so he and Justin both had a knee, at least temporarily in harmony.

"And we will never let our young'uns forget that this land was held at the price of your pa's life." He looked from Cole to Justin and rubbed a big hand over each of their heads. Except for size, the two were a matched set, both a perfect copy of their father.

Then he added, "We'll teach them to respect this ranch. It will be our children's haven, their birthright and their legacy."

ABOUT THE AUTHOR

Mary Connealy writes romantic comedies about cowboys. She's the author of THE KINCAID BRIDES, TROUBLE IN TEXAS, and WILD AT HEART series, as well as several other acclaimed series. Mary has been nominated for a Christy Award, was a finalist for a RITA Award, and is a two-time winner of the Carol Award. She lives on a ranch in eastern Nebraska with her very own romantic cowboy hero. They have four grown daughters and four precious grandchildren. Learn more about Mary and her books at:

maryconnealy.com
facebook.com/maryconnealy
seekerville.blogspot.com
petticoatsandpistols.com

The employees of Thorndike Press hope you have enjoyed this Large Print book. All our Thorndike, Wheeler, and Kennebec Large Print titles are designed for easy reading, and all our books are made to last. Other Thorndike Press Large Print books are available at your library, through selected bookstores, or directly from us.

For information about titles, please call:
(800) 223-1244

or visit our Web site at:
http://gale.cengage.com/thorndike

To share your comments, please write:
Publisher
Thorndike Press
10 Water St., Suite 310
Waterville, ME 04901